LANDOLL
Ashland, Ohio 44805

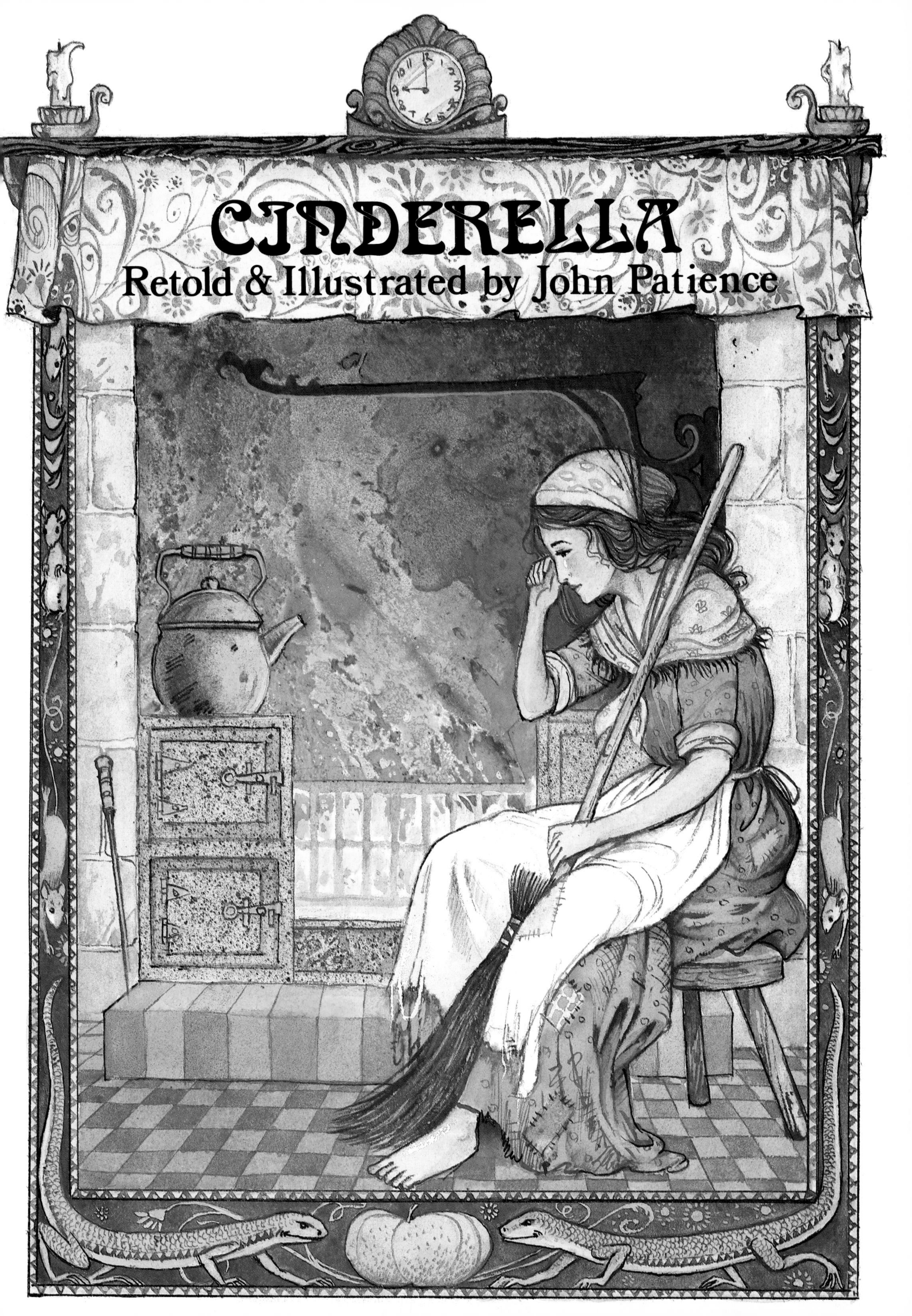
CINDERELLA
Retold & Illustrated by John Patience

"Cinderella, scrub the floor." "Cinderella, make the beds." "Cinderella, why is my dinner not ready yet?" This sort of thing was all that poor Cinderella heard from her step sisters from morning to night.

Cinderella was very beautiful and good natured but her step sisters, who were very ugly, were uncontrollably jealous of her so they made her life miserable.

One day a messenger called at the house with an invitation to a Grand Ball which the Prince was holding at the Palace. At once the step sisters were in a dither about what to wear and how they should look. "All the most handsome young men in the kingdom will be there," they cried. "We must be sure to look our best!" "Oh please can I come to the ball?" begged Cinderella. The ugly sisters howled with laughter. "You go to the ball . . . don't be so ridiculous. Just look how tattered your clothes are. You can't go looking like that, and besides, we will need you to help us get ready."

Anyone but Cinderella would have refused to help, but she was so kind hearted that she could not. On the night of the ball the ugly sisters had Cinderella running around in circles after them. "Powder my wig . . . Press my gown . . . Do this up . . . Fetch me a mirror and do hurry up you lazy creature." Cinderella felt quite dizzy by the time they were finished and she didn't even get so much as a "thank you." Her step sisters swept out to their carriage and left poor Cinderella crying quietly by the fireside.

Suddenly there was a flash of light and, to Cinderella's astonishment, a little old lady appeared. "I am your fairy godmother," she said. "Dry your eyes. You shall go to the ball. Just do as I say." First she sent Cinderella to the garden to find a pumpkin. She touched it with her magic wand and in an instant it became the most splendid coach you ever saw.

Then Cinderella was told to bring the mouse trap from the kitchen. Inside it were six white mice. The fairy godmother gave each of them a tap with her wand and turned them into snow white horses.
Next, Cinderella brought six little lizards which she found in a watering can. These were turned into six footmen with silver-buttoned coats. Finally a large black rat was transformed into a jolly coachman.

"Well now, child – you can go to the ball after all," chuckled the fairy godmother. "Aren't you pleased?" "Oh yes," exclaimed Cinderella, "But how can I go in these old rags?" At once the godmother waved her wand and the dirty old clothes were changed into a beautiful ball gown and around Cinderella's neck was a string of pearls. Then, to

complete the picture, she found a pair of dainty glass slippers on her feet. "Now, off you go and enjoy yourself," said the fairy godmother. "But remember, you must not stay a second after midnight or all your fine clothes will turn back into rags and the coach and horses, coachman and footmen will return to what they were before I worked my magic."

Cinderella arrived at the palace just as the ball was about to begin. As she entered the ballroom a murmur ran around the crowd. "Who is that beautiful girl?" The Prince could not take his eyes off her. He insisted that she dance with him for the entire evening. Cinderella had never been so happy before in her entire life. She was so happy that she didn't notice the time flying by until, suddenly, the

clock began to strike twelve. "Good heavens!" she cried, remembering her fairy godmother's warning. "I must go." She ran out into the darkness. At the twelfth stroke her fine clothes became rags and the coach turned back into a pumpkin. The Prince ran after Cinderella but she had vanished into the night. All that remained was one of her glass slippers. It had fallen from her foot as she ran down the palace steps. "I will find the girl who wore this slipper," vowed the Prince. "And I will make her my bride."

The next morning a proclamation was read out in the square to the sound of a trumpet. Every girl in the kingdom was to try on the glass slipper and whoever it fit would marry the Prince. From North and South, East and West, people came flocking to the city. Young and old, short and tall, thin and fat; one by one they tried on the glass slipper, but it fit none of them.

Eventually the slipper was brought to Cinderella's house. The ugly sisters were so excited. They snatched the glass slipper from the messenger before he could say a word. "Look! It fits me!" cried the elder sister. "Nonsense," said the younger sister. "Your heel is sticking out. Let me try it on. There it fits me like a glove." "Well, it certainly doesn't fit like a slipper!" sneered the elder one. "Your toes are bent double." "Does anyone else live here?" asked the messenger. "Everyone must try on the slipper." "Only Cinderella," replied the sisters. "But she's only a servant girl. The slipper can't possibly fit her." But the messenger insisted that even Cinderella must try on the slipper, and so she was brought from the kitchen where she had been cooking dinner. Slowly, she took the slipper and put it on. The ugly sisters gasped in amazement. "It fits," they wailed.

Then Cinderella's fairy godmother appeared and tapped her with the magic wand. Once more she was dressed in fine clothes, even more beautiful than her ball gown. "Your carriage is waiting to take you to the palace," said the fairy godmother. The Prince was overjoyed to see Cinderella again. Soon the couple were married. Everyone went to the wedding, even the ugly sisters whom Cinderella had completely forgiven for their previous unkindness.